PLAYING
SARDINES

PLAYING SARDINES

by BEVERLY MAJOR illustrated by ANDREW GLASS

SCHOLASTIC INC.

New York Toronto London Auckland Sydney

*B*ANG! The screen door slams when I come out. It's after dinner and lights are coming on in houses. Just a few lights, because most people like to sit out on their porches.

The air is heavy and sweet-smelling…like roses and cut grass…and maybe smoke from someone burning papers or having a cookout. The fireflies start to flicker as some dark thing swoops by. A bat? A night bird? It's a shape so dark and quick I can barely see it through the corner of my eye.

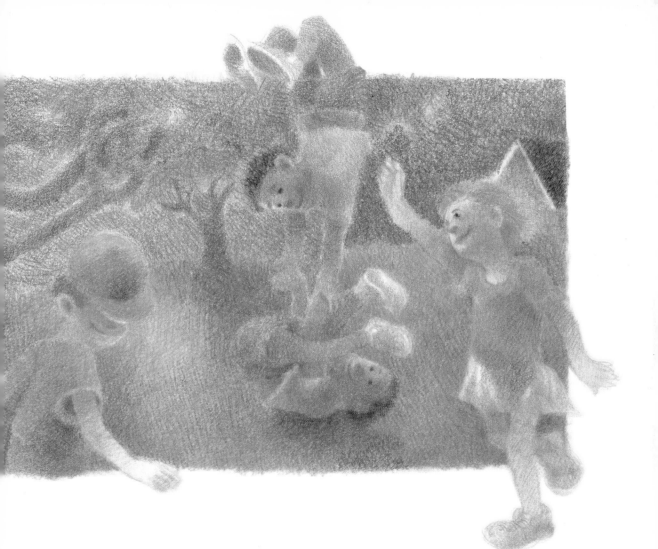

More screen doors slam, more kids come out;
my friends are ready to play. We do waiting things
like turning somersaults, climbing trees, hanging
by our knees from the branches, or making silly
faces. Then somebody says, "Let's play Sardines."

We find out who's it with a counting rhyme. "One potato, two potato, three potato, four. Five potato, six potato, seven potato, ore."

I'm it! I get to hide! All the other kids close their eyes tightly and count to one hundred. Then they yell, "Apples, peaches, pumpkin pie. Who's not ready? Holler 'I!'"

"I!" I yell loudly, so they won't come looking for me.

Now they have to count again. I want to find a very good place, the best place, the best place in the world. Here, under the forsythia bushes? They'll look there. David hid there last night. Here, in Blueboy's doghouse? Phew! It smells like wet dog in here and old, damp, used-up bones.

What about the toolshed? Perfect. I snuggle up on the burlap bags. I can see out the little cob-webby window. I can watch them try to find me.

The fun thing about playing Sardines is, when you find the hider, you all snuggle into the same hiding place. That's why you have to be careful to pick a nice, big space. Because every time a new person finds you, that person scrunches in with you. At the end, everybody is crushed in together like sardines in a can.

Floating faintly through the air, I hear, "Ready or not, here I come." The hunt begins!

It's getting darker. You can hear the tiniest sounds under the blanket of the night. Branches swish when someone pulls them aside and lets them go. You can hear the clink of someone putting dishes away in a kitchen and a faraway song on the radio. As the grass loses its daytime heat, it starts to get cool and damp. And the stars get brighter.

It's a little bit lonely hiding all by yourself. But nice lonely because you can hear all the night sounds. And you know that if you want to, you can jump up and go in your house, and your mother will give you cookies and milk. You don't, though, because everyone is looking for you.

Waiting time is a good time to think. I think about how I fell out of the cherry tree. And how I had an inchworm on my arm.

But now I'm finished thinking. I guess I'll scratch mosquito bites. I have to be quiet, so quiet. Quiet as the air before it rains.

Sometimes it doesn't take long for the first finder to come. And other times, it takes forever. So long that it's time for the little brothers and sisters to have their baths. Time for the mothers and fathers to go out to the porches and sit in the dark so the mosquitos won't find them.

Finally I hear somebody swishing through the grass. They are right outside the toolshed door! I'm barely breathing! They come in and then a hand gropes all around. I try to move just a little so the hand won't find me. Oh, no! I have to sneeze!

"Ah-choo!"

It's Stephanie. She crawls in next to me. We have to giggle a little. Very quietly, you know, so no one will hear.

When we look out the toolshed's little window, we can see the seekers, moving like shadows across the yard. Sometimes they move by bright windows, through the circles of yellow light on the grass.

The seekers run through the soft, dark air. Two of them, the twins, bump into each other! They fall down and roll in the grass. We can hear them laughing, very low.

Soon they find us…

…and in between us they squeeze.

There's the neighbor's old dog, Blueboy. He
wants to follow Amy and lick her face. He wants
to play.

Charles and Scott are looking in all the places I thought of hiding. Under the porch? No. In the garage? Oh, no. They're coming toward the tool-shed. They're standing very still. They're listening for soft, soft breathing. Jonathan bumps into the rake beside the door. Don't laugh, Stephanie! Don't breathe!

They heard us. Here they come, back to the
burlap bags in the darkest corner.

Here comes Allison. Careful, Allison! Don't fall over the lawn mower!

CRASH!

Someone else is coming, too. It's David. Now he squeezes in. Try to make room.

Sssh! Here comes another one. And another. And another. There are so many people, we can't move. We're packed in just like...just like... Sardines!

Now we hear mothers and fathers calling,
"Time to come in."
But where is Mark?

Listen! Is someone creeping around the corner? Do I see a darker shadow in the dark beside the door? Don't laugh! Don't move! Don't breathe!

We're found!

For Chris

—B.M.

*For Dorothy One
and Andrew Three*

—A.G.

ISBN 0-590-41154-3

Text copyright © 1988 by Beverly Major Schwartz.

Illustrations copyright © 1988 by Andrew Glass.

All rights reserved. Published by Scholastic Inc.

12 11 10 9 8 7 6 5 4 3 2 1   5   9/8 0 1 2 3 4/9

23

Printed in the U.S.A.